The Christmas Star

Books by Eva Ibbotson

Let Sleeping Sea-Monsters Lie . . .
and Other Cautionary Tales

Dial A Ghost
Monster Mission
Not Just a Witch
The Beasts of Clawstone Castle
The Great Ghost Rescue
The Haunting of Hiram
The Ogre of Oglefort
The Secret of Platform 13
Which Witch?

Journey to the River Sea
The Dragonfly Pool
The Star of Kazan

For older readers
A Company of Swans
A Song for Summer
Magic Flutes
The Morning Gift
The Secret Countess

The Christmas Star

A Festive Story Collection

EVA IBBOTSON

Illustrated by
NICK MALAND

MACMILLAN CHILDREN'S BOOKS

'Vicky and the Christmas Angel' and 'The Great Carp Ferdinand' were previously
published in *A Glove Shop in Vienna and Other Stories* by Century Publishing
Company Limited 1984. Reissued by Bello, an imprint of Pan Macmillan, 2014

This collection first published 2015 by Macmillan Children's Books
an imprint of Pan Macmillan
20 New Wharf Road, London N1 9RR
Associated companies throughout the world
www.panmacmillan.com

ISBN 978-1-4472-8734-6 (PB)
ISBN 978-1-5098-1782-5 (HB)

Printed and bound by CPI Group (UK) Ltd, Croydon CR0 4YY

Contents

Vicky and the
Christmas Angel

It was mid-December and a night of snow. All day the thick, soft flakes had fallen quietly, covering the blank-faced nymphs and satyrs on Vienna's innumerable fountains; blanketing the bronze rumps of the rearing horses on which dead warriors of the Habsburg Empire rode forever; giving the trees along the Ringstrasse a spare, Siberian splendour.

Sounds in the snow were muffled. The sound of carriage wheels on the cobbles, the sound of street sellers crying their wares – even the sound of church bells, so much a part of Vienna in those days before the First World War – came far more gently in the snow.

The gas-lamps threw rings of brightness into the squares, the smart shops along the Kärtner Strasse looked like stage sets. In the big apartment houses, those grand, slightly crumbling Viennese houses which look like Renaissance palaces but house simply doctors and lawyers and other self-respecting members of the bourgeoisie, the closed shutters were pierced by rays which the snow threw back in unaccustomed brightness.

One window, however, in one such apartment house, remained unshuttered so that its square of golden light went untrammelled into the dusk. It was a bathroom window and, surprisingly for a bathroom, it was occupied not by one person but by three.

The eldest of these was a girl of about eight. She sat enthroned – and literally so, for there was no doubt about her kingship – on a linen basket from which her legs, in white ribbed stockings and kid boots, stuck out at an angle, for they were a good  six inches off the floor.

Her subjects, twins about three years old, were arranged on either side of her on gigantic, upturned chamber-pots. Epically fat, seraphically golden-haired, they sat gazing upward at their sister. Only Tilda's half-swallowed thumb, Rudi's strangulated ear as he twisted a silken curl tighter and tighter round the lobe, revealed the strain they were undergoing: the strain – at that age – of totally *listening*.

Earlier in the year, listening had not been such anguish. 'Snow White,' 'Hansel and Gretel' or Vicky's own creation – the mighty but gentle giant, 'Thunder Blunder,' whose ill-mannered stomach rumbles caused the thunder which, before they knew this, had so much frightened them . . . all these were so familiar they could be understood without this terrible concentration, this agonising immobility.

But what Vicky was telling them now was different. Somehow more important; more . . . true. It was about Christmas, which was coming ('Soon, now,' said Vicky, *properly* soon'). Christmas, a concept so staggering that the twins could hardly grasp it, involving as it did everything they had ever warmed to: food and smiling people and presents – and, most mysterious of all, the *tree*.

'A *great* tree,' said Vicky. 'Mama will buy it at the Christmas Market. But it will be nothing. Just a fir tree. And then . . .'

And then . . . The twins sighed and swayed a little on their seats as Vicky told them the story that every child in Vienna knows: the story of the Christ Child who comes on Christmas Night when the children sleep, to bring the presents and decorate the tree.

But because it was Vicky, in whom the flame of imagination burnt with an almost dangerous brightness, the fat and placid twins saw more than that. They saw the gentle, tiny babe in the manger turn, on Christmas Eve, into a great golden-winged angel who flew through the starry night bearing the glittering array of baubles for the tree; heard the beating of his wings as he steadied himself; felt the curtains stir as he flew in from the mighty heavens to make *their* tree wonderful, leave *their* presents in lovingly labelled heaps beneath its beauty.

'It's the *angel* does all that?' said Tilda, removing her thumb.

'Of course. The Christmas Angel.'

'Can he carry all the presents?' demanded Rudi. 'If I get a big engine can he carry that?'

'He can do everything,' said Vicky. '*Everything*.'

5

*

But the angel in the household of Herr Doktor and Frau Fischer had help. In the kitchen Katrina, fat and warm and Czech like all the best cooks in Vienna, produced an ever-growing pile of gingerbread hearts and vanilla crescents; of almond rings and chocolate *guglhupf.* Vicky's mother, pretty and frivolous and very loving, helped too, whispering and rustling behind mysteriously

closed doors. As for Vicky's father, erupting irately from the green baize door of his study shouting, 'Bills! Bills! Nothing but bills!', he possibly helped most of all.

A week before Christmas the Christmas visitors began to arrive. First came Vicky's cousin, Fritzl, just a year older than she was, with his mother Frau Zimmermann.

Frau Zimmermann, her father's sister, was something Vicky did not understand; something called a 'Free Thinker'. It meant having to go and speak to the servants when other people were saying their prayers, and taking Fritzl to see the skeletons in the Natural History Museum when everyone else was going to hear the Vienna choirboys. Since Vicky loved both the skeletons and the choirboys, she could never decide whether Free Thinking was a good thing or not.

It was the same with Fritzl. Mostly Fritzl was her friend – inventive and talented. After all, it was Fritzl who had lowered a stuffed eel down the ventilation shaft into Frau Pollack's flat below. But at other times . . .

This time, particularly, the odd and restless side of Fritzl seemed to have got worse. He had hardly unpacked before he started telling her all sorts of things. Things which weren't actually very interesting because Kati, the washerwoman, who was her friend, had explained them to her already and anyway they were obvious enough to anyone who used their eyes. But Fritzl added other things which were to say the least of it unlikely because the Kaiser simply wouldn't have done them.

But it was in the bathroom at story time that he worried her most. During 'Snow White', or 'Daniel in the Lion's Den', or 'Thunder Blunder', Fritzl listened well enough, sitting between Tilda and Rudi with his back against the bath. But when it came to the story which mattered more than any other because literal and actual and *true* – then Fritzl made her nervous, fiddling with the loofah, tapping his feet on the tiled floor until Tilda, through her sucked thumb, said moistly and reproachfully, 'Shh, Fithl; she'th telling about the *angel*!' And even then he would sit with his dark, too-bright eyes boring into Vicky and make her go on too quickly, as though only by reaching the end of the story could she find safety. But safety from what?

The last of the Christmas visitors was Cousin Poldi.

Cousin Poldi arrived, as inevitable as the sunset, on the Friday before Christmas Eve, having travelled from Linz where she lived alone above the milliner's shop in which she worked.

Nothing, by then, could put a blight on the Christmas spirit, but Cousin Poldi usually achieved a kind of halt in the general ecstasy, making it necessary for Vicky and the twins, and even her parents, to recharge themselves so to speak after the impact of her arrival.

For Cousin Poldi was, in every way, most decidedly a 'Poor Relation'. Dressed in fusty, dusty black with button boots which looked as though the cat had spent the night on them, she wore a bracelet consisting of a sparse plait of grey hair which had been cut from the head of her mother after death. While there was nothing particularly tragic about the death of Cousin Poldi's mother, who had passed away peacefully in her bed aged eighty-six, the circumstances and the strange smell of preservative which clung to the bracelet made it an object of terror to Vicky, for whom kissing Cousin Poldi when she arrived was a minor kind of martyrdom.

And now, with everyone safely in position, the household of Herr Doktor Fischer could march forward to the great climax of Christmas Eve. A frenzied last-minute clean-up began, the maids gliding silently up and down the already gleaming parquet with huge brushes strapped to their feet. Carpets were thumped, feather-beds beaten, and in the kitchen . . . But there are no words to describe what went on in a good Viennese kitchen just before Christmas in those far-off days before the First World War.

Bed-time prayers, for the children, became a laborious and time-consuming business. Vicky, obsessed by her angel, devised long entreaties for his safe conduct through the skies. The twins, on the other hand, produced an inventory which would not have disgraced the mail order catalogue of a good department store. And each and every night their mother got them out of bed again, all three, because they had forgotten to say: 'And God bless Cousin Poldi.'

Five days before Christmas, the thing happened which meant most of all to Vicky. The tree arrived. A huge tree, all but touching the ceiling of the enormous drawing room, and: 'It's the best tree we've ever had, the most beautiful,' said Vicky, as she had said last year and the year before and was to go on saying all her life.

She wanted presents, she wanted presents very *much,* but this transformation of the still, dark tree – beautiful, but just any tree – into the glittering, beckoning candle-lit vision that they saw when one by one (but always children first) they filed into the room on Christmas Eve . . . That to her, was the wonder of wonders, the magic that Christmas was all about.

And though no one could accuse the Christ Child of having favourites or anything like that, it did seem to Vicky that when He came down to earth He did the Fischers especially proud. There never did seem to be a tree as wonderful as theirs. The things that were on it, such unbelievably delicate things, could only have been made in Heaven: tiny shimmering angels, dolls as big as a thumb, golden-petalled flowers, sweets of course – oh, every kind of sweet. And candles – perhaps a thousand candles, thought Vicky. Candles which caused her father every year to say, 'You'll see if the house doesn't catch fire, you'll see!', and which produced also a light whose softness and radiance had no equal in the world.

The twins grew less seraphic, less placid as the tension grew. 'Will the angel come tonight?' demanded Tilda at her prayers.

'No,' said Vicky. 'You've got to go to sleep for two more nights.'

'I want him to come *now*,' said Rudi, '*Now . . .*'

For the last two days, the time for the young ones passed with unbearable slowness. Even Vicky, clothed in her own mantle of imaginings, grew restless. Only Fritzl, who did not have to bless Cousin Poldi because he was not allowed to say his prayers, retained his cheerfulness.

But at last it was the twenty-third and on that night her mother turned the key in the huge double doors which led to the drawing room. And at this sound the chrysalis which had been growing inside Vicky all these days broke open and Christmas, in all its boundless and uncontrollable joy, broke out.

13

*

She had not expected to sleep but she must nevertheless have slept, because she didn't hear Fritzl come in and yet suddenly he was there bending over her in his nightshirt, shaking her.

'He's there!' said Fritzl, his voice hot and eager. 'Come on, get up. I'll show him to you.'

'Who?' she asked, still stupid from sleep.

'Who do you think? The Christmas Angel. The Christ Child. The one you're always going on about. He's in there, decorating the tree.'

Vicky sat up. Even by the subdued glow of the night-light, Fritzl could see her turn pale. 'But then . . . we shouldn't.'

'Oh, don't be so soft. We wouldn't go in. You can see quite well through the keyhole.'

So Vicky got up and felt for her slippers and crept after Fritzl down the long parquet corridor, careful to make no sound. Her heart was pounding and she felt sick, and this was all because soon now she would see a sight so blinding, so beautiful . . .

That was why she was afraid. That was the reason. Not anything else.

They were up to the door now. Fritzl was right, the key had been taken out, the hole that was left was big enough . . .

'Go on, have a look,' said Fritzl, giving her a push.

Vicky stepped forward.

'Fritzl! Vicky! How *dare* you!'

Her mother's furious voice sounded from behind them; her arm came out and wrenched Vicky away from the door.

But Vicky had already seen.

Seen the step-ladder, the bunched skirt pulled up to reveal, above the dusty button boots, a desperately unfragrant length of stocking. Seen Cousin Poldi, her mouth full of pins, reach up to hang the star on to the tree.

There was little anyone could do. Her father, frightened by her pallor, her stony silence, gave her a white powder; her mother sat by her bed

chafing her hands and wishing as she had not wished anything for years, that Vicky would cry, wail, reproach them for lying – anything to show that she was still a child. But Vicky said nothing. Nothing to Fritzl slinking off to his room, nothing to her parents. Nothing to anyone, because there was nothing at all to say.

Even so, she must have slept once more because she was woken by the sound of sobbing. Not the twins' sobbing, not a child's sobbing at all, but an ugly tearing sound. A sound which frightened her.

She got up and went on to the landing. Though she'd known really what it was, she stood for a while outside Cousin Poldi's door as though hoping for a reprieve.

Then she turned the handle and went in.

Cousin Poldi was sitting upright in a chair. Her starved looking plaits hung down on either side of her blotchy face and there was something dreadfully wrong with her mouth. On the table between the glowing, shining things: snippets of silver ribbon, wisps of gossamer lace, lay the hair bracelet, curled like the tail of some old, sick animal.

Vicky took two steps forward and stood still.

'Your mother is right,' mumbled Cousin Poldi, her hand over her mouth. 'I'm an old idiot, fit for nothing. Every year she reminds me to block up the keyhole – and then I forget.'

Vicky said nothing.

'I get excited, you see . . . All year I prepare . . . So many things are wasted in a milliner's shop, you wouldn't believe; pieces of stuff, bits of ribbon. I keep them all and then in the evenings I make things for the tree. It's a bit lonely in Linz, you see . . . It keeps one busy.'

Vicky took a sudden step back. She had seen the teeth in the glass beside the bed and understood now what was wrong with Cousin Poldi's mouth.

'Every year I've done the tree for your mother. It was so nice being able to help . . . she's so good to me, so beautiful. If it had been her you'd seen . . .' She broke off. Then forgetting her naked gums she dropped her hand and looked at Vicky with a last entreaty in her rheumy eyes.

'I've spoilt it for you forever, haven't I?' said Cousin Poldi.

And Vicky, implacable in her wretchedness, said, 'Yes.'

In every family there is apt to be a child around whom, in a given year, Christmas centres – not, of course, because that child is more greatly loved than the others, but because of something – a readiness, a special capacity for wonder, perhaps just a particular age – which gives that child the power of absolute response.

In the Fischer household that child had been Vicky. Now, with the centre dropped out of their Christmas world, Herr Doctor and Frau Fischer nevertheless had to push the day relentlessly along its course.

Fritzl, moody and ill-looking, was no help. It was the twins with their sublime unconcern, their uncomplicated greed, who made it possible to carry on; Rudi wriggling through morning mass in St Stephen's cathedral, Tilda screeching up and down the corridors waiting for dusk.

And then at last it was over, the agonising waiting, and the moment had come. The moment when they all assembled in the dining room and listened to the sweet soft tones of the old cow-bell with which their mother summoned them. The moment when the door was thrown open and, the children first, the adults afterwards walked in, dazzled, towards the presents and the tree.

With a last despairing glance at Vicky's face, Frau Fischer reached for her bell. And then: 'Stop!' said Vicky. 'We're not all here.'

Everyone looked at everyone else. 'I'm here,' said Rudi, reasonably, sticking to essentials. So were Tilda and Fritzl; so was Fritzl's mother. Herr Doktor Fischer with his home-made fire extinguisher was there; so was the cook, so were the maids.

'Cousin Poldi isn't here,' said Vicky.

Herr Doktor Fischer and his wife exchanged glances.

'She's gone, Vicky; she's going back to Linz. She thought it would be better.'

'Then she must be fetched,' said Vicky.

'But, Vicky . . .'

'We can't go in till we are all together,' said Vicky, still in that same inflexible, unchildlike voice. 'She'll have to be fetched.'

Herr Doktor Fischer took out his watch. 'The train doesn't go until four,' he said to his wife. 'I could probably get her still. But it would take some time.'

Vicky said nothing. She just stood and waited and for the first time since Fritzl had stolen to her in the night, there was a glimmer of tears in her eyes.

'You had better go,' said Vicky's mother quickly. 'We can wait.'

The word *wait* fell on the twins' heads like a cartload of boulders.

'No,' wailed Rudi, 'Rudi *can't* wait!'

'Nor can't Tilda wait neither. Tilda wants her presents now!'

'Hush,' said Vicky sternly. 'How *dare* you act like that on Christmas Eve? And anyway, I'm going to tell you a story.'

Still sniffing, doubtful, they came closer. 'In the bathroom?'

'No. Here.'

'What story do you think?' she said to the twins. 'On a day like this? The story of the Christmas Angel, of course. The one who came last night, to bring the presents and decorate the tree.'

And she told the story. Told it so that Frau Fischer had to move over to the velvet window curtain and hide her face. Told it so that the sound of Herr Doktor Fischer's footsteps, the squeak of Cousin Poldi's returning button boots, were almost an intrusion.

No one said anything. Only when at last the great doors did open and Vicky moved forward to follow Fritzl and the ecstatically tottering twins into the room, her mother held her back.

'No, Vicky,' she said softly, 'let the children go in first. We adults . . . we *adults* will come on afterwards.'

And then very slowly, she led her daughter forward towards the shining glory of the tree.

★

The Christmas Star

The story I'm going to tell you is definitely going to be a Christmas story. I mean it will have holly in it and mistletoe and so on (though also one or two other things, like a Finn, three Malawians and a lady with goose pimples). And of course a love interest, because I realized some time ago that if I wanted to earn my living by my pen it would be no good Spurning Romance. It is also a warm-hearted family saga. At least, I hope it is. You can never be absolutely certain with my family.

Actually my family has been a great disappointment to me. At the minute I'm only fifteen and busy with my O levels, but I intend to publish my first novel when I'm nineteen so that I shall still look good on the dust jacket. And of course normally I'd have relied on my home life to provide me with raw material: brooding jealousies, intolerable tensions, all that kind of thing. Instead of which my mother (who ought to be utterly *torn* about her role as a woman) is nutty about my father, who teaches biology at the local Grammar School and is not only not sexually obsessed by a Swedish au pair girl but gets terribly depressed if my mother even takes him to a Swedish *film* and only wakes up when the supporting film comes on and people start shooting each other. Then there's Tina, who's nineteen and at the university here and is *very* pretty with long, blonde hair and peat-boggish sort of eyes. Obviously what Tina ought to be doing is reacting frantically against Mum and Dad and staying out all night. Whereas what

Tina likes best is to come home early from college and watch old musicals on TV with her knitting. I suppose my brother Rickie . . . well, he *could* be torn with Freudian frustrations; there's always hope. I mean he's only eight and who knows what's going on inside him, but I must say he *seems* disgustingly ordinary. So you see what, as a sensitive feminist novelist, I am up against.

However, to return to Christmas. Christmas with us starts in the middle of November with my mother ringing up her friends, and her friends ringing up my mother. My mother has a *lot* of friends, and when Rickie and I come in from school at teatime we hear her telling them that *this* year Christmas is going to be *different*. This year they're all going to be *sensible* and *economical*, and not drive themselves mad. And then there is a long pause which is her friends telling her the same thing back.

After that comes the Christmas Row. The Christmas Row is between my mother and my father and is about how it isn't necessary for us to go bankrupt *every* year and that if my mother didn't think she was a cross between a bottomless cornucopia and Paul Getty we might hope to go on surviving into January and February or even *March*. The row ends with Dad striding out of the house and Mother *tidying* things, which she only does when she's very far gone, and is followed by the Reconciliation, which is both of them saying how foul they are and Mother deciding to economize by not sending a Christmas card to the fishmonger's son but only the fishmonger.

The next thing after that is that all of us go to the German Bazaar. And that is where this year our Christmas began to go a trifle off the rails.

The German Bazaar is run by the Lutheran Church in our town (which is a medium-sized provincial one, a bit sooty but with a wide river and ships hooting up it in the night) and we go there to get things like Advent rings (which are beautiful fir wreaths with four candles, one for each Sunday in Advent) and Advent calendars that don't have little Noddy-type characters on them but proper golden angels, and silver frosting, and stars.

This year, however, they had a big money drive on for repairs to the church, so as well as the usual stuff like gingerbread houses and embroidered aprons and cinnamon cakes there were lots of extra stalls and raffles and things.

And there was this rather plump girl in a dirndl, standing by this booth.

'Poor thing,' said my mother, 'she looks cold.'

Actually she did, in those short puffed sleeves. Also fat, and rather sad.

'Perhaps we ought to go and see what she's doing,' said my mother – at which point Father, who has a nose for trouble, bolted cravenly to the Pickled Gherkin Stall. The rest of us, however, trotted obediently along.

Well, what this cold, sad German girl was doing, it turned out, was telling fortunes. It

wasn't, she said, what she *should* have been doing. What she *should* have been doing on the last day of November (which is what this was) was standing under a plum tree waiting for a dog to bark, which was an old German custom and would tell her from what direction her future husband was due to arrive. But the town, she said, was short of plum trees and in any case she was already married to Herr König who kept the Delicatessen and so the Herr Pastor had told her to tell fortunes instead.

At which point we should all have gone firmly away, because in my view it is *fatal* to meddle with the gods, always has been, always will. However, try explaining this to my mother.

'In you go, Janey,' she said, pressing half a crown into the plump girl's hand, and pushed me into the booth.

My fortune was pretty dull. Dark men, long life, that kind of thing. One bit however was interesting. 'You shall have soon some money,' said the fat girl, the goose pimples rising like igloos on her arm. 'Very soon. Before Christmas there comes to you this money. Is gut, yes?'

I said yes, and went out to tell the others. The mention of money cheered Rickie, and when Mother handed over another half-crown and pushed him in, he went quite willingly.

'A voyage,' he said when he came out, looking extremely pleased. 'A long, *long* voyage with adventures in it. Soon. Before Christmas I shouldn't wonder.'

Then it was Tina's turn. 'Don't tell me,' said Mother when she came out. 'Wedding Bells!'

Tina nodded smugly. 'Who?' demanded my mother, who has been gunning for ages for a boy called Andy Young, who lives down the road and is training to be a musician.

'Well,' Tina said thoughtfully, 'Actually . . . a Finn.'

'A *Finn*!'

'Well, I think so. She said a handsome blue-eyed

man from a far northern land where the sea freezes in winter. I thought at first it might be a Russian, but I don't think they'd let anyone through the Iron Curtain just to marry me, do you?'

Mother said she doubted if they'd do anything so sensible and went into the booth. She was only in for a short time and when she came out she was blushing.

'Come on,' we said, 'give!'

But Mother absolutely wouldn't. I suppose it should have struck us then that something pretty odd was going on, because the difficulty with my mother isn't getting her to tell you things, it's getting her to *stop*.

I need hardly say that the matter of the fat German lady passed completely from our minds. I mean, if someone who themselves admitted that they should have been standing under a plum tree waiting for dogs to bark told *your* fortune, I doubt if you'd take much notice, especially if they were covered in goose pimples at the time.

Anyway, I was suffering very deeply with my end-of-term exams and Tina was writing terrible essays about tribes like the Hehe and the Mumu, whose customs were inclined to put her off her food. (When Tina got to university they gave her a lot of forms to fill up and when she'd finished she found she was reading Social Anthropology.) She also went to a lot of Christmas Dances with Andy Young, the music student Mother is gunning for. Meanwhile the vicar had chosen Rickie to be 'A Boy' in the Carol Service on Christmas Eve and whenever I trudged in late he was standing at the top of the stairs doing his bit of Isaiah 9: 2, 6, 7, and Dad was standing at the bottom saying, 'Don't *shout*, Rickie, project! *Project!*' which was all right except for the gaps in Rickie's teeth, which made it uncertain just *what* was going to be projected.

And then suddenly the exams were over. And on that day, as I trudged home through the last of the piled-up leaves, my foot bumped against something.

It was an old-fashioned leather purse. And inside, when I opened it, were thirty pounds in notes!

As you can imagine, I wasn't exactly pleased. I was tired and hungry and the police station was half a mile in the opposite direction. However, when I got there I had a nice surprise. The sergeant took my name and address and then he said if the purse wasn't claimed within three months it would be mine. It was extraordinary, he said, how often people *didn't* claim things, and he would let me know.

I went home dreaming of a dove-grey portable typewriter yielding to my lightest touch. But it wasn't till we were all together at tea that Rickie produced an angle that I hadn't thought of.

'Well, the goose-pimple lady was right about *you*, anyway,' he said.

35

*

Needless to say I didn't take much notice; Rickie after all is my brother. However about a week later something happened which really *did* shake me a bit.

Tina had gone to a party with Andy Young and some other friends. When Tina stays out late, Mother sits up Not Being Worried. Mother Not Being Worried is such a heart-rending sight that Dad or I usually take it in turns to go through it with her. My exams being over, it was me.

We could see there was something a bit odd about Tina as soon as she came in. She had a glazed, dreamy, rather awed look in her eyes – a look that didn't seem to be due to nice ordinary Andy Young.

'I met,' she said, 'the most *fantastic* man.'

I like to think that I knew what was coming, but actually I didn't.

'Who was he, love?' asked Mother, beaming.

36

'Well,' said Tina in rather an odd sort of voice. 'As a matter of fact, he was a *Finn*.'

She brought him to tea a couple of days later and one had to admit that Tina had not exaggerated. Niklasson Nefzelius was tall and blond with light blue eyes which seemed to reflect the unmoving waters of one of his native lakes. He was beautifully dressed, mostly in those pale, clean Scandinavian mackintoshes and in fact had no drawbacks at all except for a complete inability to speak English. This was unusual in a Finn but it was just our bad luck that Niklasson had been educated in a private school which had decided that the British were done for and had taught him a lot of other languages instead.

'What does he do?' my father enquired. 'I mean, what's his job?'

Tina pulled out a piece of paper. It had on it a large number of tubes all curled up together. They could have been sewage pipes, frankfurter sausages or some subtle chemical experiment, but what they were was Niklasson Nefzelius explaining to her what he did.

In the days that followed, Tina's dazed and glazed look persisted. She said that there was obviously more in this fortune-telling business than we believed, and even took a book out of the library on German Christmas customs. As a result of this she went to bed one night with her feet on the pillow and her head on the bottom of the bed because if you did this during Advent it was supposed to make you dream of your future husband. When she came down next morning she said she'd dreamed she was eating scrambled eggs on top of a Number Fourteen Bus.

'Who with?' demanded my mother.

Tina said she couldn't see his face but he'd been wearing a pale mackintosh and worrying about getting egg on it. After which she went off to do some Christmas shopping and Mother and I stacked the breakfast dishes in a gloomy silence because not even by the remotest stretch of the imagination could we imagine Andy Young worrying about egg on his mackintosh. Andy Young didn't *wear* a mackintosh and, if he had done, was most unlikely to worry about getting egg on it.

Meanwhile Christmas, in the way that it does, suddenly got its bit between its teeth. Mother and her friends still rang each other up but now it was to say that *next* year they wouldn't drive themselves mad. The Christmas tree arrived and got stuck in the door and Mother said that if Father was going to use language like that it made a Mockery of the Whole Festival and Tina asked three Malawians to Christmas Dinner.

It was in the middle of all this that we suddenly realized how oddly Rickie was carrying on. We'd find him crouched in the garden at night, trying to adjust his Woolworth compass by the stars, or in the bathroom rubbing vinegar into his feet to harden them. But it wasn't till Mother showed me his letter to Santa Claus that I realized what was up.

'Dear Santa,' it said, 'Please can I have some (lots) of pakets of supe and some vetamin pills and some ships biscits and if youve some money left some boots with nales in (Sined) Rickie.'

'What do you make of that, Janey?' asked my mother.

'Don't you *see*?' I said, horrified, 'The plum-tree lady said I'd find some money and I did, and she said Tina would meet a Finn and she did. So of course he thinks what she foretold for him will come true also.'

'A long voyage!' said my mother, clutching her forehead. 'Oh my God!'

The next day she went out and sold her amethyst brooch and bought a space rocket and a game of table football in addition to the pile of presents she'd already hidden for Rickie on top of the wardrobe. All the same we all knew that when you have expected to go on a Long Voyage with ship's biscuits and nailed boots, not even twenty-seven games of table football will compensate for your disappointment. And this was the way matters stood on Christmas Eve.

Christmas Eve, if you remember, was Rickie's Big Day when he was being 'A Boy' in the Carols by Candlelight Service. So at five thirty we all wrapped ourselves up and went off to church with a big box of Kleenex tissues for Mother to weep into when Rickie started on his bit of Isaiah 9: 2, 6, 7. Andy Young was playing the organ and we sang 'Unto Us a Boy Is Born' and 'O Little Town of Bethlehem' and then Rickie went forward and climbed on to the lectern. Only his head didn't nearly reach to the top and all we could see was this slither of fair hair in the dark church, and I have to admit that he hadn't got past 'The people that walked in darkness' before not just Mother but all of us were diving for the Kleenex. And it was at that point that I realized suddenly that Rickie didn't *have* to be disappointed about his voyage because it was in

my power to put things right.

Afterwards Tina went off to meet her Finn and we went home and got Rickie to bed and helped him to hang up his stocking.

When Tina returned, she looked odd. Niklasson had taken her, she said, to a Scandinavian restaurant and the waiter had brought some small white nasty drinks which was what they had in Finland to help them with the winter solstice. After that everything swam about, she said, and Niklasson had got out his dictionary and taken her hand and *drawn* things. Then she took out a piece of paper. On the paper was a picture of a girl with long hair very like Tina, and the word 'wife'. There was also the word 'yes' and the word 'no'. The word 'no' was crossed out. Tina said she thought she'd done it.

'Oh my God,' said my mother. 'Tina, you're engaged.'

Tina said she supposed she was. She said you never really *knew* about fat ladies at bazaars who ought to have been standing under plum trees and

43

she supposed it was all *meant*. She said she was sure she was going to be very happy and why was there *never* a handkerchief in this house when one needed one.

So then we opened some cooking sherry and kept telling Tina how thrilled we were, honestly, and Mother said she was sure she *would* be able to learn enough Finnish to tell her grandchildren the story of the Three Bears, it just might take a little time.

But my last memory of Christmas Eve wasn't of Tina's engagement or of us creeping in to fill Rickie's stocking. It was of Mother standing in the bathroom in her dressing gown, looking wild and distraught and dabbing eau de cologne behind her ears. 'She obviously had second sight, that woman,' she said, gazing at me unseeingly. 'It seems to me I might just as well give up struggling.' And with a last dab at the eau de cologne she tottered off towards her bed.

*

The morning of Christmas Day was beautiful and crisp and clear, with that marvellous silence you only seem to get on that particular morning. When I'd opened my own stocking, which was most satisfactory in every way, I did what I always do on Christmas Morning; I went along to Rickie's room.

The usual thing on Christmas Day is Rickie bouncing about in bed on a pile of shattered coloured paper, and a noise like thunder which is him banging and thumping and rattling with his toys.

Today no sound came from his door. When I opened it I found him lying flat on the pillow like a child in hospital. His bulging stocking was unopened, and tears were streaming down his face.

'Rickie!' I said, trying to scoop him up. 'Rickie, what's the *matter*?'

No answer. Just more tears, desperately swallowed. Then suddenly of course I knew.

'Rickie, it's *all right*,' I told him. 'You *are* going on a voyage. I *promise*!'

And I explained my plan, which was to use the money in the purse I'd found (and which still hadn't been claimed) to book him on a Children's Trip to the Continent.

Rickie continued to gulp. He said he *knew* he was going on a long voyage. Everything else the plum-tree lady had foretold had come true so obviously this would too. It just struck him as pretty unusual, he said, for boys of eight to be *sent* on long voyages. Most people, he said, wanted to keep their boys at *home* when they were only eight years old. They liked to look *after* such boys, he said, and not push them out to places where they would get smashed up and eaten by crocodiles and miss the pantomime.

'You mean . . . Rickie, you don't *want* to go on this voyage?'

Rickie said that wasn't what he meant *at all*. He wanted to go on a long voyage *very much*. Only *later* when he was a proper age, like eighteen or something. After which he burst into tears again and said he wanted his mum.

Well, that was easy. I hauled him out and shoved him into my parents' room and Mother said he must be mad to think she'd let him out of the *house* let alone on a Long Voyage when we all depended on him so much, and Dad said he'd personally thump anyone who tried to take his son anywhere for at least ten years. Then Mother said had he liked his stocking and Rickie said actually he hadn't opened it because he knew it was packets of soup and things and he'd keep it till he was eighteen. And Mother said did he really think Santa was so completely *thick* as to fill the stocking of an eight-year-old boy with packets of soup and would he please fetch it at *once* and bring it in. So that was all right.

I was just going back to my room to put on some clothes when the doorbell rang. I was on the landing, but even so Tina got down first in her totally useless white broderie anglaise dressing gown, and it was Andy Young saying 'Happy Christmas' and giving her a bunch of Christmas roses.

I don't know if everyone is the same as I am about Christmas roses. Maybe it's the legend of how they originated, springing out of the snow the night that Jesus was born, or maybe it's just *them*: all those pale, uncoloured petals and delicate green veins. Anyway, I find Christmas roses somewhat *moving* and it must have been the same with Tina, because she took them and immediately burst into tears.

Needless to say this had a devastating effect on Andy, who turned pale, put an arm round her and said he promised *never* to bring her Christmas roses again only would she *please* stop crying. So Tina said it wasn't the Christmas roses but being properly engaged to a Finn and being in an awful *muddle*, and Andy was just taking his arm away and looking stricken when the bell rang again and it was the Finn.

'Wife!' said the Finn happily, grabbing Tina by the arm. 'Wife! Yes!'

And: 'Yes! Yes! Here I haf come!' said a lusty voice from behind him and out stepped a big blonde, long-haired girl, beaming all over her face. 'You haf said I can come for the Christmas Feeding, yes? That is the English Hospitality! Thank you. Yesterday I haf flowed here in the aeroplane. How good you haf been to my Niki!' said Mrs Nefzelius.

If anyone tells you that Scandinavians are cold, don't listen to them. Mrs Nefzelius kissed me and

49

kissed Tina and kissed Andy. She kissed Mother and Rickie and would have kissed Dad only he got away, and when the three Malawians came, she kissed them. We had a terrifically gay Christmas Dinner and afterwards we lit the Advent ring and Mrs Niki pounced on it and put it on her head, flaming candles and all, which is what they do in Finland, like the Germans stand under a plum tree waiting for dogs to bark, and the Malawians nodded happily and said, 'Very English is this Christmas. Very English.' And I know you will not be surprised to hear that at this point the telephone rang and it was the police sergeant to say he was extremely sorry but an old lady who'd been laid up with pneumonia had claimed my purse.

'That poor, *silly* plum-tree woman,' said Tina later, '*didn't* she mess it all up!'

We'd got to the best bit of Christmas: the bit where everyone except the family has gone home (only Andy stayed; I guess he's going to *be* the family) and you've put a handful of pine needles on the fire to scent the room, and everyone's relaxed and peaceful.

Father said that was hardly surprising. The only effect fortune telling had ever had, he said, was on the minds of credulous idiots like ourselves. There could never be any *practical* effects, he said, because it was all bunkum from beginning to end.

Mother said she hoped so. She hoped so very much. And then, at last, she told us what the plum-tree lady had foretold for *her*.

'Of course I didn't believe it at first,' she said. 'But then when everything else seemed to be coming true . . . I just . . . well, I suppose I just gave in, you know how one does. But I expect it'll be all right.'

'I don't,' said Father in a voice of unspeakable gloom.

And as so sadly and so often happens, Father was right. Not that we mind, really, now that we're sort of used to the idea. As we keep telling each other when morale looks like cracking, the new baby'll be company for Rickie. But one thing is certain: next Christmas, at the German Bazaar, no one in this family is moving *one step* from the Pickled Gherkin Stall!

★

The Great Carp Ferdinand

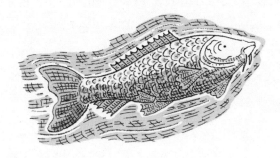

This is a true story, the story of a Christmas in Vienna in the years before the First World War. Not only is it a true story, it is a most dramatic one, involving love, conflict and (very nearly) death – and this despite the fact that the hero was a fish.

Not any fish, of course: a mighty and formidable fish, the Great Carp Ferdinand. And if you think the story is exaggerated and that no fish, however mighty, could so profoundly affect the lives of a whole family, then you're wrong. Because I have the facts first-hand from one of the participants, the 'littlest niece' in the story, the one whose feet, admittedly, failed to reach even the first rung of the huge leather-backed, silver buttoned dining-room chairs, but whose eyes cleared the table by a good three inches so that, as she frequently points out, she saw it all. (She came to England, years later, this littlest niece, and became my mother, so I've kept tabs on the story and checked it for accuracy time and again.)

The role the Great Carp Ferdinand was to play in the life of the Mannhaus family was simple, though crucial. He was, to put it plainly, the Christmas dinner. For in Vienna, where they celebrate on Christmas Eve and no one, on Holy Night, would dream of eating meat, they relish nothing so much as a richly-marinated, succulently roasted carp. And it is true that until you have tasted fresh carp with all the symphonic accompaniments (sour cream, braised celeriac, dark plum jam) you have not, gustatorily speaking, really lived.

But the accent is on the word *fresh*. So that when a grateful client with a famous sporting estate in Carinthia presented Onkel Ernst with a live twenty-pounder a week before Christmas, the Mannhaus family was delighted. Onkel Ernst, a small, bandy-legged man whose ironic sympathy enabled him to sustain a flourishing solicitor's practice, was delighted. Tante Gerda, his plump, affectionate wife, was delighted. Graziella, their adorable and adored eighteen-year-old daughter, was delighted, as was Herr Franz von Rittersberg, Graziella's 'intended', who loved his food. Delighted too, were Tante Gerda's three little nieces, already installed with their English governess in readiness for the great Mannhaus Christmas, and delighted were the innumerable poor relations and rich godfathers whom motherly Tante Gerda collected every Christmas Eve to light the candles on the great fir tree, open their presents and eat . . . roast carp.

Accommodation for the fish was not too great

a problem. The house in Vienna was massive and the maids, simple country girls accustomed to scrubbing down in wooden tubs, cheerfully surrendered the bathroom previously ascribed to their use.

Here, in a gargantuan mahogany-sided bath with copper taps which gushed like Niagara, the huge, grey fish swam majestically to and fro, fro and to, apparently oblivious both of the glory of his ultimate destiny and the magnificence of his setting. For the bathroom was no ordinary bathroom. French tea roses – marvellous, cabbage-sized blooms – swirled up the wallpaper, were repeated on the huge china wash-bowl and echoed yet again in the vast chamber-pot – a vessel so generously conceived that even the oldest of the little nieces could have sunk in it without a trace.

And here to visit him as the procession of days marched on towards Christmas came the various members of the Mannhaus family.

Onkel Ernst came, sucking his long, black pipe

with the porcelain lid. Not a sentimental man, and one addicted to good food, he regarded the carp's ultimate end as thoroughly fitting. And yet, as he looked into the marvellously unrevealing eye of the great, grey fish, admired the gently-undulating whiskers (so much more luxuriant than his own sparse moustache), Onkel Ernst felt a distinct sense of kinship with what was, after all, the only other male in a houseful of women. And as he sat there, drawing on his pipe, listening to the occasional splash as the carp broke water, Onkel Ernst let slip from his shoulders for a while the burden of maintaining the house in Vienna, the villa in Baden-Baden, the chalet on the Wörther See, the dozen or so of Gerda's relatives who had abandoned really rather early, the struggle to support themselves. He forgot even the juggernaut of bills which would follow the festivities. Almost, but not quite, he forgot the little niggle of worry about his daughter, Graziella.

Tante Gerda, too, paid visits to the carp – but

briefly, for Christmas was something she could never trust to proceed even for a moment without her. She came hung about with lists, her forehead creased into its headache lines, deep anxieties curdling her brain. Would the tree clear the ceiling – or, worse still, would it be too short? Would Sachers send the meringue and ice-cream swan in time? Should one (really a worry, this) 'send' to the Pfischingers, who had not 'sent' last year but had the year before? Oh, that terrible year when the Steinhauses had sent a basket of crystallized fruit at the very last minute, when all the shops were shut, and she had had to rewrap the potted azalea the Hellers had given and send it to the Steinhauses – and then spent all Christmas wondering if she had removed the label!

Bending over the fish, Tante Gerda pondered the sauce. Here, too, was anxiety. Celeriac, yes, lemon, yes, onion, yes, peppercorns, ginger, almonds, walnuts – that went without saying. Grated honeycake, of course, thyme, bay, paprika and dark plum jam. But now her sister, writing from Linz, had suggested mace . . . The idea was new, almost revolutionary. The Mannhaus carp, maceless, was a gastronomic talking point in Vienna. There were the cook's feelings to be considered. And yet . . . even Sacher himself was not afraid to vary a trusted recipe.

The carp's indifference to his culinary environment was somehow calming. She closed her eyes for a second and had a sudden, momentary glimpse of Christmas as existing *behind* all this if only she could reach it. If she could just be sure that Graziella was all right. And she sighed, for she had never meant to love anyone as much as she loved her only daughter.

Franz von Rittersberg also came to see the carp. A golden-haired, blue-eyed, splendid young man, heir to a coal-mine in Silesia, the purpose of his visit was strictly arithmetical. He measured the carp mentally, divided it by the number of people expected to sit down to dinner, estimated that his portion as the future Mannhaus son-in-law was sure to be drawn from the broader, central regions – and left content.

And escaping from the English governess, scuttling and twittering like mice, white-stockinged, brown-booted, their behinds deliciously humped by layers of petticoat, came the little nieces clutching stolen bread rolls.

'Ferdinand,' whispered the youngest ecstatically, balancing on the upturned, rose-encrusted chamber-pot. Her sisters, who could see over the sides of the bath unaided, stood gravely crumbling bread into the water. The fish was a miracle; unaware of them, yet theirs. *Real*.

Each night, when the nursemaid left them, they tumbled out from under the feather bed and marshalled themselves for systematic prayer. 'Please God, make them give us something that's *alive* for Christmas,' they prayed night after night after night.

But it was Graziella, the daughter of the house, who came most frequently of all. Perched on the side of the bath, her dusky curls rioting among the cabbage roses on the wall, she looked with dark, commiserating eyes at the fish. Yet, though she was by far the loveliest of the visitors, Ferdinand's treatment of her was uncivil. Quite simply, he avoided her. Carp, after all, are *fresh*-water fish, and he had noticed that the drops which fell on him when she was there were most deplorably saline.

She was a girl the gods had truly smiled upon – loving and beloved; gay and kind, and her future as Frau Franz von Rittersberg was rosily assured. And yet each day she seemed to get a little thinner and a little paler, her dark eyes filling with ever-growing bewilderment. For when you have been accustomed all your life to giving, giving, giving, you may wake up one day and find you have given away yourself. And then unless you are a saint (and even, perhaps, if you are) you will spend the nights underneath your pillow, trapped and wretched, licking away the foolish tears.

And so the days drew steadily on, mounting to their climax – Christmas Eve. Snow fell, the tree arrived, the last candle was lit on the Advent ring. The littlest niece, falling from grace, ate the chimney off the gingerbread house. The exchange of hampers became ever more frenzied. The

Pfischingers, who still had not sent, invaded Tante Gerda's dreams . . .

It was on the morning of the twenty-third that Onkel Ernst and his future son-in-law assembled to perform the sacrificial rites on the Great Carp Ferdinand.

The little nieces had been bundled into coats and leggings and taken to the Prater. Graziella, notoriously tender-hearted, had been sent to Rumpelmayers on an errand. Now, at the foot of the stairs stood the cook, holding a gargantuan earthenware baking dish – to the left of her the housemaids, to the right the kitchen staff. On the landing upstairs, Tante Gerda girded her men – a long-bladed kitchen knife, a seven-pound sledgehammer, an old and slightly rusty sword of the Kaiser's Imperial Army which someone had left behind at dinner . . .

In the bathroom, Onkel Ernst looked at the fish and the fish looked at Onkel Ernst. A very slight sensation, a whisper of premonition, nothing more, assailed Onkel Ernst, who felt as though his liver was performing a very small *entrechat*.

'You shoo him down this end,' ordered Franz, splendidly off-hand. 'Then, when he's up against the end of the bath, I'll wham him.'

Onkel Ernst shooed. The carp swam. Franz – swinging the hammer over his head – whammed.

The noise was incredible. Chips of enamel flew upwards.

'Ow, my eye, my eye!' yelled Franz, dropping the hammer. 'There's a splinter in it. Get it OUT!'

'Yes,' said Onkel Ernst. 'Yes . . .'

67

He put down the sword from the Kaiser's Imperial Army and climbed carefully on to the side of the bath. Even then he was only about level with Franz's streaming blue eye. Blindly, Franz thrust his head forward.

The rest really was inevitable. Respectable, middle-aged Viennese solicitors are not acrobats; they don't pretend to be. The carp, swimming languidly between Onkel Ernst's ankles found, as he had expected, nothing even mildly edible.

It was just after lunch that Onkel Ernst, dry once more and wearing his English knicker-bockers, received in a mild way guidance from above.

It was all so easy, really. No need for all this crude banging and lunging. Simply, one went upstairs, one pulled out the plug, one went out locking the door behind one. And waited . . .

A few minutes later, perfectly relaxed, Onkel Ernst was back in his study. He was not only holding the newspaper the right way up, he was practically *reading* it.

The house was hushed. Franz, after prolonged ministrations by the women of the family, had gone home. The little nieces were having their afternoon rest. The study, anyway, had baize-lined double doors. Even if there *were* any thuds – thuds such as a great fish lashing in its death agony might make – Onkel Ernst would not hear them.

What he did hear, not very long afterwards, was a scream. A truly fearful scream, the scream of a virtuoso and one he had no difficulty in ascribing to the under-housemaid, whose brother was champion yodeller of Schruns. A second scream joined it and a third. Onkel Ernst dashed out into the hall.

The first impression was that the hall was full of people. His second was that it was wet. Both proved to be correct.

Tante Gerda, trembling on the edge of hysteria, was being soothed by Graziella. The English governess, redoubtable as all her race, had already commandeered a bucket and mop and flung herself into the breach. Maids dabbed and moaned and mopped – and still the water ran steadily down the stairs, past the carved cherubs on the banisters, turning the Turkish carpet into pulp.

The enquiry, when they finally got round to it, was something of a formality since the culprits freely admitted their guilt. There they stood, the little nieces, pale, trembling, terrified – yet somehow not truly repentant-looking. Yes, they had done it. Yes, they had taken the key out from behind the clock; yes, they had unlocked the bathroom door, turned on the taps . . .

Silent, acquiescent, they waited for punishment. Only the suddenly-descending knicker-leg of the youngest spoke of an almost unbearable tension.

Graziella saved them, as she always saved everything.

'Please, Mutti? Please, Vati . . . So near Christmas?'

70

*

Midnight struck. In the Mannhaus mansion, silence reigned at last. Worn out, their nightly prayer completed, the little nieces slept. Tante Gerda moaned, dreaming that the Pfischingers had sent a giant hamper full of sauce.

Presently a door opened and Onkel Ernst in his pyjamas crept softly from the smoking room. In his hand was an enormous shotgun – a terrible weapon some thirty years old which had belonged to his father – and in his heart was a bloodlust as violent as it was unexpected.

Relentlessly he climbed the stairs; relentlessly he entered the bathroom and turned the key behind him. Relentlessly he took three paces backwards, peered down the barrel – and then fired.

Graziella, always awake these nights, was the first to reach him.

'Are you all right, Papa? Are you all right?'

Only another fearful volley of groans issued from behind the bolted door. Tante Gerda rushed

71

up, her grey plait swinging. 'Ernst, *Ernst*?' she implored, hammering on the door. '*Say* something, Ernst!'

The English governess arrived in her Jaeger dressing-gown, the cook . . . Together the women strained against the door, but it was hopeless.

'Phone the doctor, the fire brigade. Send for Franz, quickly,' Gerda ordered. 'A man – we need a *man*.'

The governess ran to the telephone. Bur Graziella, desperate, threw her fur cape over her nightdress and ran out into the street.

Thus it was that in the space of half a minute the life of Sebastian Haffner underwent a complete and total revolution. One minute he was free as air, easy-going, a young man devoted to his research work at the University – and seconds later he was a committed, passionate fanatic ready to scale mountains, slay dragons and take out a gigantic mortgage on a house. For no other reason than that

Graziella, rushing blindly down the steps into the lamplit street, ran straight into his arms.

Just for a fraction of a second the embrace in which Sebastian held the trembling girl remained protective and fatherly. Then his arms tightened round her and he became not fatherly – not fatherly at all. And Graziella, with snowflakes in her hair, looked up at the stranger's kind, dark, gentle face and could not – simply could not – look away.

Then she remembered and struggled free. 'Oh, please come!' she gabbled, pulling Sebastian by the hand. 'Quickly. It's my father . . . The carp has shot him.'

Instantly Sebastian rearranged his dreams. He would visit her regularly in the asylum, bring her flowers, read to her. Slowly, through his devotion, she would be cured.

'Hurry, please, please! He was groaning so.'

'The carp?' suggested Sebastian, running with her up the steps.

'My father. Oh, come!'

Maids moaned at the foot of the stairs. Tante Gerda sobbed on the landing.

Sebastian was magnificent. Within seconds he had seized a carved oak chair and begun to batter on the door. Quite quickly, the great door splintered and fell. At Sebastian's heels they trooped into the bathroom.

Onkel Ernst sat propped against the side of the bath, now groaning, now swearing, his hand on his shoulder which was caked with blood. Round him were fragments of rose-encrusted china and shattered mirror which the lead shot ricocheting from the sides of the bath and grazing Onkel Ernst's shoulder, had finally shattered. The carp, lurking beneath the water taps, appeared to be asleep.

'Ernst!' shrieked Tante Gerda and dropped on her knees beside him.

'Bandages, scissors, lint,' ordered Sebastian, and Graziella fled like the wind.

It was only a flesh wound and Sebastian, miracle of miracles, was a doctor, though the kind that worked in a lab. Quite soon Onkel Ernst, indisputably the hero of the hour, was propped on a sofa, courageously swallowing cognac, egg yolk with vanilla, raspberry cordial laced with *kirsch*. The family doctor arrived, pronounced Sebastian's work excellent, stayed for cognac too. The fire brigade, trooping into the kitchen, preferred *slivovitz*.

And upstairs, forgotten, seeing nothing but each other, stood Graziella and Sebastian.

This was it, then, thought Graziella, this wanting to sing and dance and shout and yet feeling so humble and so *good*. This was what she had never felt and so had nearly thrown herself to Franz as one throws a bone to a dog to stop it growling. . . As if in echo to her thoughts, the bell shrilled yet again and Franz von Rittersberg was admitted. His eye was still swollen and his temper not of the best.

'This place is turning into a madhouse,' he said, running up the stairs. 'Do you know what time it is?'

Graziella did not. Time had stopped when she ran into Sebastian's arms and years were to pass before she quite caught up with it again.

'Well, for heaven's sake let's finish off this blasted fish and get back to bed,' he said, shrugging off his coat and taking out a knife and a glass-stoppered bottle. 'I've brought some chloroform.'

'No!'

Graziella's voice startled both men by its intensity. 'In England,' she said breathlessly, 'in England, if you hang someone and it doesn't work . . . if the rope breaks, you let him live.'

'For goodness' sake, Graziella, don't give us the vapours now,' snapped Franz. 'What the devil do you think we're going to eat tomorrow, anyway?'

He strode into the bathroom. 'You can help me,' he threw over his shoulder to Sebastian, who had been standing quietly on the half-lit landing. 'I'll pull the plug out and pour this stuff on him. Then you bang his head on the side of the bath.'

'No,' Sebastian stepped forward into the light.

'If Miss . . . if Graziella does not wish this fish to be killed, then this fish will not be killed.'

Franz put down the bottle. A muscle twitched in his cheek. 'Why you . . . you . . . Who the blazes do you think you are, barging in here and telling me what to do?'

Considering that both men came from good families, the fight which followed was an extraordinarily dirty one. The Queensberry rules, though well-known on the Continent, might never have existed. In a sense of course the outcome was inevitable, for Franz was motivated only by hatred and lust for his Christmas dinner, whereas Sebastian fought for love. But though she was almost certain of Sebastian's victory, Graziella, sprinkling chloroform on to a bath towel, was happily able to make sure.

Dawn broke. The bells of the Stephan's Kirche pealed out the challenge and the glory of the birth of Christ.

77

In the Mannhaus mansion, Graziella slept and smiled and slept again. Onkel Ernst, propped on seven goose-feather pillows, opened an eye, reflected happily that today nothing could be asked of him – no carving, no wobbling on stepladders, no candle-lighting – and closed it again.

But in the kitchen Tante Gerda and the cook, returning from Mass, faced disgrace and ruin. Everything was ready – the chopped herbs (bravely, the cook had agreed to mace), the wine, the cream, the lemon . . . and upstairs, swimming strongly, was the centrepiece, the *raison d'être* for days of planning and contriving, who should have been floating in his marinade for hours already.

As though that was not enough, as they sat down to breakfast there was a message from Franz. He was still unwell and would not be coming to dine with them. It took a full minute for the implication of this to reach Tante Gerda and when it did, she put down her head and groaned. 'Thirteen! We shall be thirteen for dinner! Oh, heavens! Gross-

Tante Wilhelmina will never stand for that!'

But fate had not finished with Tante Gerda. The breakfast dishes were scarcely cleared away when the back-door bell rang and the maid returned struggling under a gigantic hamper.

'Oh, no . . . NO!' shrieked Tante Gerda.

But it was true. Now, at the eleventh hour, with everything still to do and the shops closing fast, the Pfischingers had 'sent'.

*

And now it was here, the moment for which all these weeks had been the preparation. It was dusk. The little nieces boiled and bubbled in their petticoats, pursued by nursemaids with curling-tongs and ribbons. Inside 'the room', Tante Gerda, watched complacently by Onkel Ernst, climbed up and down the step-ladder checking the candles, the fire-bucket, the angle of the silver star. Clucking, murmuring, she ran from pile to pile of the presents spread on the vast white cloth beneath the tree. Graziella's young doctor, summoned from the laboratory, had agreed to come to dinner so that they wouldn't be thirteen. He had even somehow contrived presents for the little nieces – three tiny wooden boxes which Tante Gerda now added to their heaps.

And now all the candles were lit and she rang the sweet toned Swiss cow-bell which was the signal that they could come in.

Though they had been huddled straining against the door, when it was opened the little nieces came slowly, very slowly into the room, the myriad candles from the tree shining in their eyes. Behind them came Graziella, her head tilted to the glittering star and beside her the young doctor – who had given her only a single rose.

And suddenly Tante Gerda's headache lifted, and she cried a little and knew that somehow, once again, the thing she had struggled for was there Christmas.

You'd think that was the end of the story, wouldn't you? But my mother, telling it years later, liked to go on just a bit further. To the moment when the little nieces, having politely unwrapped a mountain of costly irrelevancies, suddenly burst into shrieks of ecstasy and fulfilment. For, opening Sebastian's wooden boxes, they found, for each of them, a tiny, pink-eyed, living mouse.

Or further still. To the family at table – white damask, crystal goblets, crimson roses in a bowl. To the little nieces (the youngest wobbling fearfully on her pile of cushions), each pocket of each

knicker-leg bulgy with a sleepy, smuggled mouse. To Onkel Ernst magnificent in his bandages, and Graziella and Sebastian glowing like comets . . . To the sudden stiffening, knuckles whitening round the heavy spoons, as Tante Gerda brought in the huge silver serving-dish.

And the sigh of released breath, the look of awed greed as she set it down. Egg-garnished, gherkin-bedecked, its translucent depths glittering with exotic fishes and tiny jewelled vegetables, the celebrated concoction quivered gently before them. Lampreys in aspic! Truly – most truly, the Pfischingers had 'sent'.

The littlest niece, when she grew up and became my mother, liked to end the story there. But I always made her go on just a little further. To the day after Christmas. To the house of the Pfischingers on the other side of Vienna. To Herr Doktor Pfischinger, a small, bald, mild little man ascending the stairs to his bathroom. He is carrying a long-bladed knife, a sledgehammer, a *blunderbuss* . . .

★

About the Author

Eva Ibbotson was born in Vienna, but when the Nazis came to power her family fled to England and she was sent to boarding school. She became a writer while bringing up her four children, and her bestselling novels have been published around the world. Her books have also won and been shortlisted for many prizes. *Journey to the River Sea* won the Nestlé Gold Award and was runner-up for the Whitbread Children's Book of the Year and the Guardian Children's Fiction Prize. *The Star of Kazan* won the Nestlé Silver Award and was shortlisted for the Carnegie Medal. *The Secret of Platform 13* was shortlisted for the Smarties Prize, and *Which Witch?* was runner-up for the Carnegie Medal. *The Ogre of Oglefort* was shortlisted for the Guardian Children's Fiction Prize and the Roald Dahl Funny Prize. Eva Ibbotson died peacefully in October 2010 at the age of eighty-five.

About the Illustrator

Nick Maland studied English and Drama at university and went on to work in the theatre, acting and directing. During this time he also developed an interest in drawing, which soon became a full-time occupation. He has worked as an illustrator for the *TES*, *The Times*, the *Observer*, the *Guardian* and the *Independent*, among others, as well as illustrating children's books.

He has won many awards, including the V&A Illustration Award in 2003 for *You've Got Dragons*, the Silver Medal in the Society of Illustrators: The Original Art exhibition, the Stockport Children's Book Award for *Snip Snap!* and the Booktrust Early Years Award for his work on *Oliver Who Travelled Far and Wide* by Mara Bergman.

He lives in Brighton with his wife, son and daughter.